Dear Parents,

Welcome to the Scholastic Reader series. We have taken over 80 years of experience with teachers, parents, and children and put it into a program that is designed to match your child's interests and skills.

Level 1—Short sentences and stories made up of words kids can sound out using their phonics skills and words that are important to remember.

Level 2—Longer sentences and stories with words kids need to know and new "big" words that they will want to know.

Level 3—From sentences to paragraphs to longer stories, these books have large "chunks" of texts and are made up of a rich vocabulary.

Level 4—First chapter books with more words and fewer pictures.

It is important that children learn to read well enough to succeed in school and beyond. Here are ideas for reading this book with your child:

- Look at the book together. Encourage your child to read the title and make a prediction about the story.
- Read the book together. Encourage your child to sound out words when appropriate. When your child struggles, you can help by providing the word.
- Encourage your child to retell the story. This is a great way to check for comprehension.
- Have your child take the fluency test on the last page to check progress.

Scholastic Readers are designed to support your child's efforts to learn how to read at every age and every stage. Enjoy helping your child learn to read and love to read.

—**Francie Alexander**
Chief Education Officer
Scholastic Education

For Isobel Louise — welcome
R.I.

To Sarah and Sam
K.M.

Originally published in the UK under the title *Titchy Witch and the Wobbly Fang* by Orchard Books UK.

Published by Scholastic Inc.
SCHOLASTIC, CARTWHEEL BOOKS, and associated logos are trademarks and/or registered trademarks of Scholastic Inc.

ISBN 0-439-78450-6

10 9 8 7 6 5 4 3 2 1 06 07 08 09 10

Printed in the U.S.A. 23
First Scholastic printing, March 2006

Wanda Witch and the Wobbly Fang

Rose Impey ★ Katharine McEwen

Scholastic Reader — Level 3

SCHOLASTIC INC.
New York Toronto London Auckland Sydney
Mexico City New Delhi Hong Kong Buenos Aires

Wanda Witch
Victor
Eric
Wendel
Weeny Witch
Witchy Witch
Cat-a-bogus

Wanda Witch had a wobbly fang. It wibble-wobbled all the time and she didn't like it. "Yuck!"

"Leave it alone," said Cat-a-bogus. "It will come out when it's good and ready."

Wanda Witch couldn't wait for that.

She and Dido tried to pull it out.

But the fang just wasn't ready.

Wanda Witch wanted a spell
to make it fall out.
But Dad was busy in his workshop...

. . . and Mom said, “What would the Fang Fairy say?”

Wanda Witch didn’t know about the Fang Fairy.

"When a fang comes out," Witchy Witch told her, "you put it under your pillow. Then, if you're good, the Fang Fairy brings you a surprise."

Wanda Witch loved surprises.
She wanted hers this minute.

She decided to make a spell
of her own.
"Come on, Dido," she said.
"This should be easy-breezy."

As soon as Mom was out of the way, Wanda Witch borrowed a few magic ingredients.

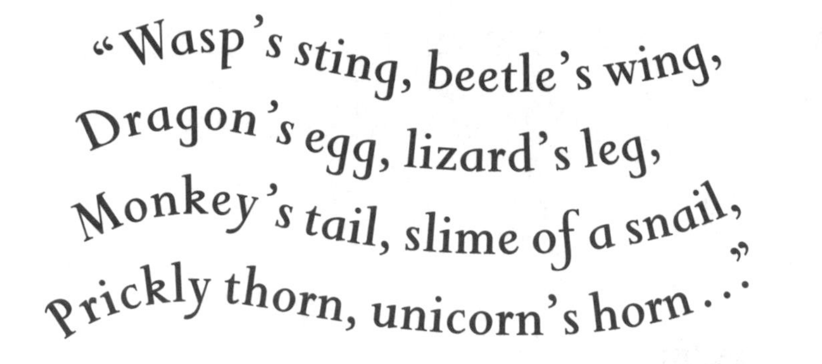
"Wasp's sting, beetle's wing,
Dragon's egg, lizard's leg,
Monkey's tail, slime of a snail,
Prickly thorn, unicorn's horn . . ."

Wanda Witch thought that should be enough.

Dido thought it might be too much!

Then she said some special magic words: "Hocus pocus,
Bim Bala Bang,
Please pull out..."

Wanda Witch was about to say,
"This wobbly fang."
But she had an even better idea.

Mom said the Fang Fairy would bring one surprise present for each of her fangs.
How many presents would she bring for all of her fangs?

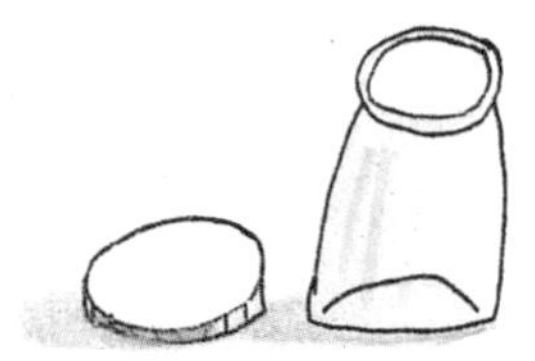

Wanda Witch started again:

"Hocus pocus,
Bim Bala Bang,
Please pull out
all of my fangs..."

Clitter, clatter, clitter, clatter.
A whole set of little fangs fell out and rolled around on the kitchen floor.

Wanda Witch looked a bit funny with no fangs.

Dido thought she looked a bit scary.

But Wanda Witch wasn't too worried . . .

…until Cat-a-bogus called her for tea.

It was hard eating termites on toast without any fangs.

Wanda Witch was keeping very quiet, too. The cat soon knew something was wrong.

Cat-a-bogus was mad. In fact, he was furious.

He made Wanda Witch empty her pockets.

Then the cat made some magic of his own. Most of the fangs went back.

All except one, which wibble-wobbled a bit. Then it kept on falling out.

The next day, Wanda Witch found a new dollar coin under her pillow. That would buy lots of chocolate grobblies.

And she still had lots more fangs to go.

Fluency Fun

The words in each list below end in the same sounds.
Read the words in a list.
Read them again.
Read them faster.
Try to read all 15 words in one minute.

born	**busy**	**decided**
horn	**easy**	**presented**
thorn	**ready**	**started**
torn	**scary**	**toasted**
worn	**wobbly**	**wanted**

Look for these words in the story.

minute	**ingredients**	**enough**
thought	**special**	

Note to Parents:

According to *A Dictionary of Reading and Related Terms*, fluency is "the ability to read smoothly, easily, and readily with freedom from word-recognition problems." Fluency is necessary for good comprehension and enjoyable reading. The activities on this page include a speed drill and a sight-recognition drill. Speed drills build fluency because they help students rapidly recognize common syllables and spelling patterns in words, and they're fun! Sight-recognition drills help students smoothly and accurately recognize words. Practice these activities with your child to help him or her become a fluent reader.

—**Wiley Blevins,**
Reading Specialist